Praise for

They Didn't Teach THIS in Worm School!

"Lia's understated visual humour goes
hand in hand with joyfully surreal adventures"
Guardian

"Laugh-out-loud and full of wonderfully
funny illustrations ... a must-read for
anyone with a sense of adventure"
Red Reading Hub

"Marcus and Laurence are hugely loveable
characters and this beautifully illustrated book
will carry you swiftly to its sweet conclusion"
Booktrust

"Sprinkled with funny illustrations and lots of laughs"
South Wales Evening Post

"A comedy classic that will have
readers wriggling with laughter"
WorldBookDay.com

"It's as hilarious as a chicken in a cat suit"
The Phoenix

"This is a gentle, touching story with many laugh-out-
loud moments and plenty of expressive pictures."
Primary Times

The Secret Time Machine and the Gherkin Switcheroo

The Secret Time Machine and the Gherkin Switcheroo

Simone Lia

WALKER
BOOKS

First published in Great Britain 2019 by Walker Books Ltd
87 Vauxhall Walk, London SE11 5HJ

10 9 8 7 6 5 4 3 2 1

Printed and bound in China

British Library Cataloguing in Publication Data:
a catalogue record for this book is available from the British Library

ISBN 978-1-4063-6347-0

www.walker.co.uk

For my darling AJ

Chapter One

It's me, Marcus.

Hmm...

I don't mean to be rude, but have we met before? In case we haven't, let me tell you a little bit about myself. My name is Marcus and I'm a worm.

Pleased to meet you

As far as worms go, I'm quite ordinary. I love digging holes in the mud, wriggling, eating, beatboxing and dreaming about potatoes. Most of these hobbies are not *that* unusual.

One of the things about me that *is* different is that I don't live in the ground. I live in a house in a tree with a big, fat bird called Laurence.

Laurence is my best friend. I don't know many other worms who live in a birdhouse. Actually, I know exactly zero worms who live in a birdhouse.

If I'm honest with you, I wasn't too sure about Laurence when I first met him.

Are you going to eat me?

The day we met he *insisted* I travel with him on an epic journey to Kenya. I wasn't that keen to go, but flying to a distant land with a bird who looked a bit like a chicken was a lot better than being eaten by one.

It was only after having a long and adventurous journey that I got to know him. Neither of us expected to become such excellent friends. I ended up moving into his house so that we could be together every single day. At first, everything was brilliant. We'd have picnics near the motorway or we'd wear butterfly costumes or we'd

BLEEP
BLEEP

HELLO
HELLO

pretend to be robots that had gone wrong and spend the whole day talking backwards.

No two days were ever the same. But when Laurence discovered a new and very dull hobby, he didn't want to do anything interesting any more. He didn't even want to leave the house. These days he sits on the sofa every waking hour like a great big blob of mashed potato with his new favourite thing: crossword puzzle books. It's SO boring!

Since he became a crossword puzzle fan, EVERYTHING has changed...

Chapter Two

Laurence was sitting in his favourite spot with his head buried in his book. He had ginger biscuit crumbs in his feathers and his beak was crusty from yesterday's parsnip soup.

"I'm stuck on a clue," he moaned. He was *always* stuck on a clue.

"Read it out," I sighed.

"*Farm animal.* Three letters beginning with P."

"*Pig.*"

"You're so good at crosswords, Marcus!" he cheered as he wrote the letters carefully in the boxes.

"I'm much better at digging!" I shot back. "Can we go outside and make a tunnel?"

"No, thanks," he said politely. "It's raining. Let's have a stay-at-home day today."

"Aw! We stay at home *every* day. It's been AGES since we've gone out and had any fun. You *never* want to do anything I want these days."

He put his pen down in a huff. "That's not fair. I'm a bird, and birds don't like being underground. How would *you* feel if I made you do something that worms don't like doing?"

You made me fly to Kenya with you

I whispered in a small voice without moving my lips.

15

"I heard that, Marcus. That was completely different. We didn't even know each other properly then. Here's another clue," he said, changing the subject back to crosswords.

"I'm not telling you the answer until you agree to coming outside."

Laurence looked worried. He half closed his book. "Do you want to do this jigsaw instead?" He held up a box with a picture of a dog carrying a basket of kittens and flowers.

"No," I said grumpily, even though it looked really good. "I want to play outside."

Laurence closed his eyes to think for a moment. "How about if you go out to play and I watch you from up here? I'll be able to see you if I lean out of the window."

I shook my head. "It's not the same."

He sighed heavily. "OK, I'll come with you."

Even though he didn't seem keen on the idea, this was the first time he'd agreed to leave the birdhouse in ages.

"I'll need to wear a special outfit, though, so I won't get mud on my feathers," he added. He waited a few seconds before saying, "What a shame we don't have anything suitable in the wardrobe. We'll just have to stay at home instead."

I flopped down from my chair. He wasn't going to wriggle out of it that easily. "*I'll* MAKE something for you, Laurence. I just need bin bags, sticky tape and a jar of gherkins."

"What do you need the jar of gherkins for?"

"To eat while I'm working on your outfit."

"Fine," Laurence grumbled. "I'll get the things you need." He stood up slowly. A piece of cheese sandwich that had been tucked in his feathers fell to the floor. He dragged his feet in slow motion towards one of the cupboards.

17

I felt annoyed and sorry for Laurence at the same time. "We don't *have* to go outside if you don't want to," I said without thinking.

"Oh, all right then," he chirped, dropping the roll of bin bags on the floor and hopping back to the sofa at great speed.

I was cross with myself for speaking without thinking. Sometimes I wished I had a special machine that would let me undo the stupid things I'd just said. A bit like a time machine. If I had one of those, I'd use it a lot!

Laurence read out another clue. "*Fruit from a tree*, five letters, second letter P."

"*Apple*," I sighed.

He wrote the letters in the boxes, whistling from his beak as he breathed. I could feel my blood pressure rising. Why couldn't he breathe properly like a normal bird?

I wondered what it would be like to have an actual time machine. There would be so much we could do with it! I'd definitely use it to stop Laurence from taking up crosswords as a hobby. And then we could go back eighty million years dressed as robots. *That* would totally confuse the dinosaurs!

coo-eee

Laurence interrupted my thoughts as he loudly snorted to clear his nasal beak passages. Did he really have to make such horrible noises ALL the time? He was always clearing his beak or whistle-breathing or stirring his mug of hot chocolate and making a *clink clink clinkity clink* sound. It was SO annoying.

Klaghem

clag
clag clag
aghem

CLINK
CLINK
CLINK

Also, since he'd adopted the habit of being boring and lazy and sitting on the sofa all day, he'd stopped taking his regular bird baths and now he smelled like a sweaty goat. No offence to goats. I shook my head crossly; I'd just about had enough of Laurence with his disgusting smells and irritating noises!

"What are you thinking about?" Laurence asked cheerfully as he stirred a mug of hot chocolate, making a *clink clink clinkity clink* sound.

"NOTHING," I answered abruptly. I couldn't tell him what I was thinking, it was too horrible.

"It looked as though you were deep in thought."

"I was thinking about a time machine," I said in a panic.

"What time machine?"

I blurted out the first thing that came into my head. "The one that my auntie built."

"Your auntie hasn't built a time machine," he retorted rudely.

"Yes, she has," I insisted, even though she hadn't. I was annoyed that he didn't believe me. I closed my eyes and continued, "My auntie has travelled throughout history in it."

Laurence's beak was wide open. "But time machines haven't been invented, Marcus."

"I told you already," – I sighed at having to repeat myself – "my auntie built one. She invented them."

He sat up straight on the sofa. "Has she really?"

I nodded, smiling proudly. "She certainly did." I was excellent at lying.

"Can we go and see it and travel into the past?"

I hadn't thought that far ahead, so I sat there for ages like a worm statue thinking of what to say.

"Are you OK, Marcus? You look funny."

"Yes, I'm fine; I was just thinking about what we might eat for dinner."

"Can we go and see it?" Laurence asked again.

"Definitely, yes." I didn't know what else to say.

Laurence stood up and clapped his wings above his head while wiggling his hips. The rest of his cheese sandwich fell from his armpit onto the floor. It smelled like it had been in there for ages.

THUD

"I'm going to have a bath to celebrate."

"At last!" I cheered joyfully.

Laurence looked upset.

"I mean, at last … you'll get to see my auntie's invention. You're going to love it."

"I will!" He hopped to the bathroom. "I can't believe you didn't mention this before! We can go as soon as it stops raining."

"I can't wait!" I called out.

At last we were going to leave the birdhouse and breathe some fresh air. I wish I'd lied about my auntie having a time machine ages ago.

I lay down on the floor and looked at the ceiling and made a mental list of all the things I needed to do before we left the house. I just needed to:

A - Find out how time travel works

B - Build a time machine without Laurence noticing

C - Do A and B before it stopped raining.

It probably wouldn't be too difficult to do all of that...

tick tock
tick tock
tick tock

Chapter Three

Building a time machine was going to be a lot trickier than I'd first imagined. Even though Laurence had been in the bath for ages, I hadn't had a single idea how to do it. I didn't even understand how time travel worked. I was pretty sure they hadn't taught us *that* at worm school.

A panicky feeling rose through my worm body. I needed to invent something before it stopped raining. The sun loomed behind a rain cloud; it could beam its way out at any moment and ruin everything.

I paced backwards and forwards; it was difficult to concentrate with the grandfather clock ticking so loudly. Even wearing Laurence's socks on my head did nothing to muffle the *tick-tock*ing. Everything was going wrong!

"Are you all right?"
Laurence asked suspiciously.

"I'm completely fine," I
said, shaking off my ear
socks. He blew his beak
noisily with a spotty
handkerchief and hopped
into the bedroom.

I circled the room at great speed, hoping it
might get my brain juices flowing.

It didn't work.

Perhaps I'll have an idea if I sit somewhere
different, I thought.

"Are you *sure* you're
all right?" It was
Laurence again. He
looked worried.

I tried to convince him. "Yes, I feel exactly the same as I felt a minute ago. Never better."

"Oh … OK then," he stuttered before shuffling into the kitchen.

As soon as his back was turned I frantically swung round and round while hanging from the lampshade to activate my worm brain. And then it happened – a brilliant thought popped into my head.

Laurence had a huge collection of books. He would DEFINITELY have something in his library that explained how to build a time machine. I dropped and rolled to the shelves with glee. There were books on history, travel, learning German, knitting, steamrollers, science, tree house design, cake baking, advanced electromagnetic field theory and quilt making, to name but a few. But I couldn't find any books about time machines.

I was about to start panicking again, when
I wondered what kind of books a very clever
inventor-type person would read if they wanted to
build a time machine.

"Probably science books," I said out loud by
accident.

"What are you doing?" Laurence asked as he
came back out of the kitchen. He had a sandwich
and four mini chocolate rolls piled on his plate.

"I'm choosing a book to read."

Laurence looked very, very concerned now.
"But you don't like reading."

I ignored him and pulled out a large book on quilt making. "This one looks good." I didn't want him to guess that I was doing research for my invention.

"Are you totally and utterly sure you're feeling OK? I can fetch the thermometer and take your temperature if you like?"

Laurence asking me how I was feeling every five minutes was making me hot and sweaty. Perhaps I *wasn't* well after all.

"I've never felt better," I lied. "I'm going to sit quietly and read this. I've always wanted to learn how to sew a patchwork quilt."

"All right then." He seemed to believe me.

As he hopped to the sofa, I sneaked a science book into *Quilt Making for Beginners* and flicked through the pages.

There was a chapter on something called quantum physics that explained time travel.

EINSTEIN THEORY OF RELATIVITY

← Albert Einstein

THE maths...

$$R_{\mu\nu} - \tfrac{1}{2} R g_{\mu\nu} + \Lambda g_{\mu\nu} = \tfrac{8\pi G}{c^4} T_{\mu\nu}$$

or

$$G_{\mu\nu} = R_{\mu\nu} - \tfrac{1}{2} R g_{\mu\nu}$$

and then...

"I'm going to learn everything there is to learn about quantum physics," I muttered with joy. Fortunately Laurence was too busy eating his sandwich to hear me.

It said that for time travel to be possible, you needed to move faster than the speed of light. This could be a problem. I only had a bicycle, and I didn't think it would be able to go *that* fast, even with Laurence pedalling down the massive hill near our house.

Then something caught my eye. There was a bit about a scientist called Albert Einstein, who a long time ago said that time travel could be possible through a thing called a "wormhole". I couldn't believe it! I'm a worm: I dig holes!

The wormhole in the book

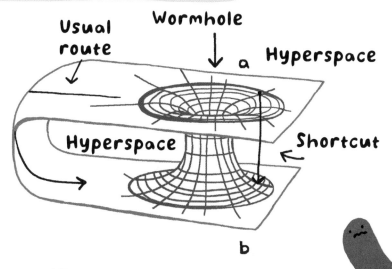

Usual route

Wormhole

a

Hyperspace

Hyperspace

Shortcut

b

The wormholes in the picture didn't look anything like the holes I dig, though. They were in outer space. How would I get *there* on my bike? As I continued, I read that scientists didn't even know whether wormholes existed.

What's the point of that then?

I grumbled out loud.

"What did you say, Marcus?" Laurence's face was smeared with blobs of hummus from his sandwich.

"Oh, um, I was saying that this quilt has very delicate needlepoint."

Laurence didn't reply. I felt cross with Albert Einstein for being so clever. I slammed the book shut. I was *really* cross with Laurence too. If it wasn't for him not wanting to play outside with me, I wouldn't have to trick him into leaving the house by going to the trouble of inventing and building a time machine.

SLAM!!!

It was all too difficult. I didn't want to be an inventor any more. I wanted to do something that *I* enjoyed and that *I* knew how to do.

I've had enough!

Of reading about quilts?

"No. Of EVERYTHING. I'm going to play in the mud all by myself."

Laurence looked taken aback. "But it's raining."

"I LIKE the rain!" I shouted as I wriggled across the floor. I wanted to swing the front door wide open to make a dramatic exit but I couldn't reach the handle, so Laurence had to come and open it for me.

He poked his head out to speak to me on the porch. "Would you like me to give you a lift to the bottom of the tree?"

"Yes, please," I whispered.

Chapter Four

Laurence lowered his neck for me to slide down to the ground. "Have a nice time digging," he said kindly.

"I *WILL*!" I blurted in an angry yet tuneful way before wriggling off. I didn't even look round to watch him fly back up to the tree house. Instead I stuck my head straight in the mud and tunnelled down.

It felt like heaven being in the soft cool earth again. *This is where I belong*, I thought as I burrowed deeper and deeper. I didn't have to worry about anything when I was underground. But even though I was doing my favourite thing, too many thoughts were popping up in my worm brain. I was worried.

What would I do when I'd finished digging? If I went home, Laurence would still be waiting to visit my auntie's time machine.

I couldn't tell him that it didn't exist. He'd be upset and disappointed that it was all a lie. And then we'd be back at square one, doing crosswords and Laurence never wanting to leave the house.

If I didn't go home, where would I go? Would I have to stay underground for ever? The thought made me shudder. I'd really miss Laurence and the birdhouse *and* that jar of unopened gherkins that needed eating.

I lay down and moaned loudly, "Why can't I be as clever as Albert Einstein? I wouldn't have *any* problems then."

Why?

I felt truly sorry for myself for having such a small worm brain. Hoping it might make me feel better, I started to dig a great big worm tunnel.

When I'd finished, I was very surprised
to see that I'd accidentally made
something quite spectacular.

It was the best tunnel I'd ever built.
"Ha! I bet Albert Einstein couldn't have
done that!" I chuckled out loud to myself. *And
I bet he couldn't have made something like this...*

Perspiring, I stopped to look at what I'd made. It was possibly the most enormous worm tunnel that had ever been dug by a single worm. I'd never seen anything like it, not even in the *Guinness Book of Worm Records*. A warm glow of pride ran through me.

"I think I might be an actual genius – a worm-tunnelling genius!" I marvelled out loud.

I stopped to take in the greatness of what I had just achieved. It felt brilliant being exceptionally good at something. And then I remembered that there are a lot of things I am good at. I paused to make a list in my mind...

ALL THE THINGS I'M REALLY GOOD AT:

- Digging tunnels
- Wriggling
- Knowing the answers to Laurence's crossword puzzles
- ~~Lying~~ Making up imaginative stories
- Doing sums in my head
- Pretending to be a baguette
- Not being eaten by a bird for breakfast
- Gherkins (eating them)
- Sort of flying to Kenya
- Beatboxing
- Going to the toilet
- Sometimes having interesting dreams
- Sitting on a chair
- Talking
- Not talking
- Looking out of the window

```
        0 0 0 3 2 4 · 0 2
579 ⟌ 1 8 , 7 6 0 9 · 0 0
      - 0
        1 8
      - 0
        1 8 7
```

My worm body tingled. Perhaps I was even cleverer than Albert Einstein. Why hadn't I noticed before? Why hadn't anyone else noticed? I felt like I had been reborn. Everything seemed different, more straightforward somehow.

I laughed at how the *old me* had struggled to understand quantum physics. Now I knew I was a genius, I would go back and study that book again. It would be easy. I'd make the time machine and I'd probably even have time to sew myself a beautiful quilt as well.

I sighed with happiness and started to tunnel back up to the surface of my massive tunnel. When I popped my head up above the soil, I was surprised to see that instead of being surrounded by the familiar trees next to the birdhouse, I was in the middle of a circle of unfriendly-looking bird beaks.

Perhaps I wasn't so clever after all. Clearly I had taken a very wrong turn.

Chapter Five

Not this again, I thought as I dangled from the beak of a bird.

He flung me up in the air. I had to think quickly. The only thing that might save me from being eaten was if I did the same as when I first met Laurence and tried to engage him in a friendly conversation.

"HAVE YOU GOT ANY BROTHERS OR SISTERS? DO YOU PREFER DOGS OR CATS? WOULD YOU RATHER BE ABLE TO SNEEZE PICKLED ONIONS OR CRY MILK CHOCOLATE TEARS?"

But the bird wasn't interested in talking. Instead he tottered about to find the right position to catch and swallow me up.

This is it, I thought. I tensed my worm body and closed my eyes tightly as I plunged towards his wide-open beak.

47

Just then I heard a vaguely familiar voice calling out, "Hold on, Bernard. Isn't that Marcus?"

It was too late: I'd landed.

I wasn't sure if I was still alive. I opened one eye and then the other, half expecting to be surrounded by angels in worm heaven. There were no angels, but there were the same birds who had been there two seconds before. I glanced up and saw that I was nestling in the wings of Bernard. I knew Bernard. He was one of Laurence's neighbours. Instead of eating me, he'd caught me.

"Are you all right?" he asked. "I didn't realize it was you! You were going to be my mid-morning snack."

"I'm fine, thank you," I said, relieved. It was reassuring to see him and other familiar faces.

"How *are* you and Laurence?" Shakira, another of Laurence's neighbours, asked. "We were just saying the other day how we haven't seen you two out and about for ages."

My worm body became tense again. I didn't
want to tell her all the problems I was having with
Laurence. I'd have to explain how we stayed at
home all the time doing boring crosswords and that
he hadn't been bothering to take showers and how
annoyed I'd been with him because he whistled
when he breathed and I'd lied about my auntie
having a time machine and I'd gone off in a grump
because I didn't understand quantum physics and
I thought I might have been a genius but really I
wasn't and I didn't know what I was going to do.

I didn't say anything.

Shakira looked worried. "Has something happened to him?"

She wasn't getting the hint that I didn't want to talk, so I tried changing the subject and said, "Is that the time?" while looking at an imaginary watch on my imaginary wrist.

Shakira looked very worried now and was clutching her wings to her face. "We haven't seen Laurence for weeks and now you're acting strangely. My bird instincts are telling me something terrible has happened to him."

I didn't want to disappoint her bird instincts so I made something up. "Well, since you ask," I sighed, "a few weeks ago, Laurence was flying around the woods and he bumped his head on a branch and fell all the way to the ground."

It wasn't a very interesting story but everyone seemed gripped and they all gasped at the same time in horror.

"Is he all right?"

"You know what he's like; he doesn't complain." I was enjoying having everyone's attention, and added more details to the story. "He's been at home in bed with a bump on his head. I've been looking after him day and night, reading him stories and making him parsnip and lentil soup."

"Oh no, poor, poor Laurence," Shakira said.

51

Bernard gave me a tight hug before putting me on the ground. "You're such a good friend, looking after him like that. And to think I almost ate you, Laurence's selfless and kind-hearted worm friend," he said remorsefully, giving his chest a gentle thump.

A little part of me felt a bit guilty about lying, but the other part felt wonderful that the birds believed my story and thought that I was Laurence's kind and selfless friend.

"Is there anything we can do to help? Shall we visit him? Bring him food? Serenade him from outside his window?"

"He just needs quiet rest at home and to be left alone," I said quickly, not wanting them to visit and see that he was perfectly fine. "He's much better than he was, and the bump is getting smaller."

"Let us know if there's anything that we can do," Shakira said. All of the birds were looking at me with their huge kind eyes. An unexpected thought came to me; maybe they *could* help...

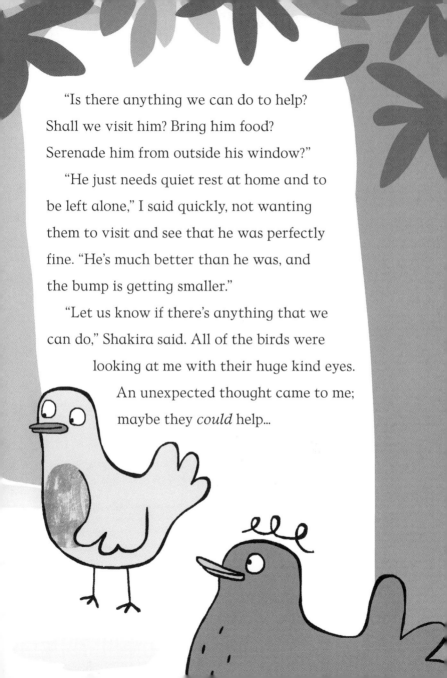

"There is one thing that would definitely make things better."

"What is it?" Bernard asked.

The bird gathering drew in closer. "What is it? We'll do anything for him."

"I don't know if you'll be able to do it; it's asking a lot..."

"Tell us what it is!"

"Well, ever since Laurence banged his head, he's been having some very strange thoughts. I don't know *where* he got this ridiculous idea from but he seems to think that my auntie has built a time machine."

"A *time machine*?"

"Yes, that knock on the head must have affected his brain a *lot*. This 'time machine' is all he ever talks about, and he'd do anything to see it. I can't bring myself to tell him that it doesn't actually exist."

"How can *we* help?" one of the birds asked cautiously.

"Well," I said, casually, "if you could just find a way to build a working time machine and let him have a go in it, I'm pretty sure he'd be very happy."

The group took a step back in surprise. A few birds began muttering.

"But that's impossible!"

"We can't do that."

"Time travel hasn't even been invented!"

"This is absolutely ludicrous."

It wasn't long until everyone was moaning and groaning. Then someone piped up with a firm "HUSH!" from the back of the group.

Everyone fell silent and made room for the bird to hop forward. "Just what are you all thinking?! You've been talking about a bird who you say is your friend, who at this very moment is home in bed with a poorly head. It's a disgrace how you are all saying that it's impossible. Laurence travelling in a time machine is the *very* least we can do."

"But *how* can we do it, Vera?" Bernard whispered.

Vera ignored him and looked at me with determined eyes. "*Nothing* is impossible. I've got this, Marcus." She put her wing on her heart and held it there.

I gazed at her in awe. "Do you think you could arrange it for when it stops raining?" I asked softly.

"Yes," she replied in an even softer voice, and then she pivoted on one foot and hopped away with her wings outstretched. "Laurence's dreams are about to come true!" she cried dramatically.

No one said anything. I had worm goose pimples. Maybe Vera was some kind of magical time-travelling bird wizard. I didn't know who or what she was but I really wanted to believe her.

"Shall I give you a lift back to your house, Marcus?" Shakira whispered.

"Yes, please," I said, grateful for the offer as I wasn't sure where I was.

Everything was working out beautifully. I was getting a lift home and Vera was going to sort out all my problems.

Nothing could go wrong.

Chapter Six

"Sorry I went off in a bit of a grump," I said to Laurence when he opened the front door.

He picked me up and gave me a hug. "It's good to see you, my friend. It was too quiet here without you."

I was glad to be home. The grandfather clock was *tick-tock*ing, the smell of baking was wafting from the oven and Laurence had loads of lumpy crumbs in his feathers.

"Have you been eating biscuits?" I asked, nibbling on a morsel.

"A whole packet," he admitted, putting me on the floor and then patting himself down. "I'll do some star jumps later. How was your digging?"

"It was really good." I wanted to tell him that Bernard almost ate me by accident but I decided not to. If I told him that, I'd have to tell him about Shakira and how I'd made up a story about him bumping into a branch and getting a mind-altering blow to the head. I was beginning to lose track of the lies I'd told that day, and the guilty feeling was rising in me again. I imagined swallowing it down so that it would go away.

"Would you like a hot chocolate and a slice of home-made cheese and leek pie?"

"There's nothing I'd like more," I replied enthusiastically. I hoped the cheese and leek pie would make my guilty feelings go away. "Some gherkins would go down nicely too," I added,

thinking that might help as well.

"I'll bring the jar!" Laurence said merrily, hopping to the cupboard.

We had a cosy night in that evening, eating pie and doing crosswords together. Laurence did loads of star jumps and I accidentally ate the whole jar of gherkins. I also made that jigsaw, the one with the dog carrying a basket of kittens and flowers.

After almost being eaten that
day, it didn't seem so
bad staying at home
in the warm, dry,
cosy birdhouse with
Laurence. It was certainly
a lot safer. I wondered why
I'd been so keen to go out before. A part of me
thought Laurence probably had the right idea
about staying home all the time. Why go out
when everything you need is right there?

I decided that first thing in the morning I would explain to Laurence that there wasn't really a time machine. I'd made it up. Then we could stay at home every day for the rest of our lives. He'd definitely understand.

That night I listened to the *pitter patter* of gentle rain on the birdhouse roof as I fell asleep. Apart from having a stomach ache from eating too many gherkins, everything was perfect.

Chapter Seven

The sun filtered through the curtains of the bedroom window, gently waking me from a dream about a gherkin that was singing a sad song about a kitten. I did a satisfying waking-up stretch and yawn and then caught a whiff of a heavenly aroma wafting from the kitchen.

Hurrah! It must be Saturday. I smell pancakes! I thought to myself. Laurence always made blueberry pancakes at the weekend as a special treat.

"Guess what day it is today?!" he announced as he burst through the bedroom door.

"It's blueberry-pancake-a-day!" I said in a sing-song voice.

"It is! And also" – he hopped onto his bed and whipped open the curtains – "it's the day we travel in your auntie's time machine! Look, it's stopped raining!"

SWOOSH

SWOOSH

The warm, bright, horrible sunshine flooded every inch of the room, hurting my eyes.

I had to tell Laurence the truth before he got his hopes up too much.

"I CAN'T WAIT; I CAN'T WAIT!" he squealed as he bounced up and down on the bed.

Too late. Laurence was already too excited. I definitely didn't want to tell him now; he'd be really disappointed and it would all be my fault. I had to think of a way to let him down gently.

"Let's go straight after breakfast!" he exclaimed, clapping his wings together.

My head was hurting from worrying about what to do. I didn't want to tell Laurence *another* lie.

"I don't feel very well," I said. This wasn't *exactly* a lie because my head actually *was* aching. "I'm not sure if I can go out today, or tomorrow, or ever."

"What's wrong?" Laurence asked, looking both worried and disappointed at the same time. He rested his wing on my forehead to check my temperature.

"I've got a sore throat," I croaked in my scratchiest voice. This *was* a lie, but a headache didn't quite sound ill enough.

"Oh NO!" he said. "You sound *terrible*." He tilted his head to one side. "It's strange – you sounded fine a minute ago when you were looking forward to your pancakes."

"I know – it came on *so* quickly. You'd better go without me," I sighed, knowing full well that he was far too kind to leave me on my own.

"I couldn't possibly leave you on your own," he protested, putting his wing to his breast. "I'll make you a honey and lemon drink and look after you until you get better."

He hopped into the kitchen. I could hear him putting the kettle on the stove and washing up the frying pan. I mostly felt relieved that we wouldn't be going, but I was also experiencing that pesky guilty sensation again. I swallowed it down so that I wouldn't need to think it. Funnily, doing that made me feel like I actually did have a real sore throat.

"Ooh! What's this?" Laurence was squealing again. He hurried back to the bedroom. "This was under the front door," he said, waggling a blue envelope in my face. "It's a letter! The first letter I've *ever* received."

Laurence
Laurence's house
1 Oak tree
Oak Tree Woods

"Who's it from?" I asked curiously as he ripped it open.

"I don't know. It looks like some kind of invitation."

"Read it out," I said, remembering just in time to make my voice all raspy.

Laurence didn't say anything; his eyes were wide open.

"What is it?"

"Nothing," he said, stuffing the card back into the envelope. "Drink your honey and lemon."

"Is it something horrible?" I asked.

"No. It's something brilliant, but … it doesn't matter. Let's just get you feeling better again."

"Tell me what it is!"

He looked at me. "I think it's from your auntie." Laurence took the card out of the envelope again and slowly read it aloud.

Laurence and Marcus are cordially invited to view the only TIME MACHINE in the world. Enclosed are two return tickets for one journey.

Only valid today.

Meet the Keeper of the Key at 10 a.m. at the secret location.

PS Marcus knows where the secret location is. (It's where we were yesterday.)

Vera had only gone and done it! She'd magicked up a time machine with her amazing powers of wizardry. I had butterflies and rainbows dancing in my belly!

"We're going to see the time machine!" I cheered.

"But we *can't*," Laurence said firmly. "You've got a sore throat."

I'd forgotten about that. I cleared my throat. "I feel better now! It's gone away again!" I said, throwing the covers off my bed. "We'd better get going; we don't want to be late."

"Are you sure?"

"Yes, that honey and lemon really did the trick." I gave a little cough. "See! That was the last of it! It's all gone. Let's eat our breakfast. Come on!"

Laurence punched the air and bounced on the bed a few more times.

We ate our pancakes so quickly that we didn't even remember to enjoy them. And in our haste we left all the dishes in the sink and the beds unmade.

We both went to the toilet, and just as Laurence was about to open the front door he said that he felt weird going out without making his bed. So we went back, made the beds, and washed, dried and put away the dishes. Laurence did a bit of light dusting, then vacuumed the house. We went to the toilet again, and then we were ready to leave.

Neither of us knew what to expect next.

Chapter Eight

Down a bit

It had been ages since I'd flown with
Laurence. I'd forgotten how cosy it was
snuggled in his soft feathers. We soared
freely above silent treetops in the gentle
breeze. The only sound to be heard
was my voice calling out the
directions. It was blissful
flying again.

Loop the loop a bit

As we approached the secret location, Laurence let out a shrill cry. "THERE SHE IS! THERE SHE IS! I THINK I CAN SEE YOUR AUNTIE!" He made a speedy nosedive with a clumsy running landing, narrowly missing a bird on the ground.

My heart skipped a beat with excitement and relief to see that the bird was Vera.

She composed herself hastily and smiled serenely.

"Greetings," she said softly. "You must be Laurence and you must be Marcus." She was acting as if she didn't know me. I tried to follow her lead.

"I have no idea who you are; we've definitely not met before."

"I am Vera, Keeper of the Key." She pulled out a key on a large ring from her feathers.

Laurence held his feathery wing tips to his cheeks. "Is that for the time machine?" he gasped.

She nodded solemnly. "Yes. Today you shall both embark on a genuine time-travelling adventure." She dangled the key hypnotically in front of Laurence's beak. "Have you brought your invitation?"

"Yes," Laurence replied slowly, following the swinging key with his gaze.

Vera stared fixedly at both of us and then bent down towards some long branches lying on the ground. As she swept them to one side, a huge great big hole was revealed. It took me a moment to realize that it was the massive worm tunnel I had dug yesterday.

"What's that?" Laurence asked, screwing up his face in puzzlement.

"This," she announced grandly, "is a wormhole."

Laurence looked less than impressed.

"A *wormhole?*"

"Indeed," Vera explained. "But it's no ordinary wormhole. It's not for worms; it's for time travelling. It's the only existing time-travelling portal on this planet. The time machine is down there."

Vera shone her torch into my fantastic wormhole.

"WOW!" Laurence gasped with excitement.

"Ssshhh." Vera put her wing fingers to her beak. "No one except me – and now you – knows that any of this exists. It must ALWAYS remain a secret."

Laurence was jumping up and down now, and trying unsuccessfully to be quiet as he giggled uncontrollably. I couldn't quite believe what was happening. Without even trying, it seemed I'd made an actual time-travelling portal. Perhaps I was a genius after all. I was excited but also a little bit scared.

"We must go in before anyone sees us," Vera ordered, glancing around.

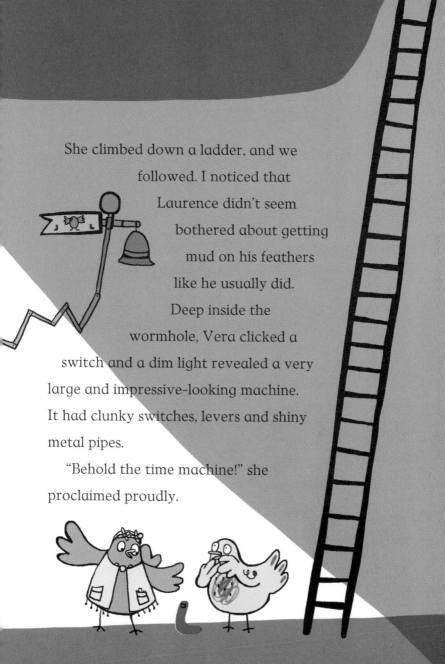

She climbed down a ladder, and we
followed. I noticed that
Laurence didn't seem
bothered about getting
mud on his feathers
like he usually did.
Deep inside the
wormhole, Vera clicked a
switch and a dim light revealed a very
large and impressive-looking machine.
It had clunky switches, levers and shiny
metal pipes.

"Behold the time machine!" she
proclaimed proudly.

"It's beautiful," Laurence said with awe, stroking the machine with his wing.

"DON'T TOUCH IT!" Vera asserted in a bold voice.

Laurence quickly whisked his wing away as if he'd touched a piping hot jam tart.

"It's important that you don't touch *anything*."

Laurence apologized. I was half scared and half full of admiration for Vera. I wanted to touch a lever so that she'd tell *me* off too. But before I had a chance, Vera ushered us towards two seats at the front of the machine.

"Strap yourselves in here," she ordered.
"We're almost ready for take-off."

"Where are we going?" Laurence asked with
a big goofy smile on his face.

Vera shone the torch under her beak so that
we could see her clearly. It was very dramatic.
"You'll be going back in time hundreds of
years."

"This is amazing!" Laurence whispered
loudly to me.

I nodded. "It really is."

We heard a key being turned and a mechanical clunk as a dial was rotated.

"Something's happening," Laurence said, shuffling in his seat.

"The machine is powering up!" Vera called from behind us.

Things began to shake and rattle. It felt a bit like someone behind us was jiggling the machine backwards and forwards. Laurence and I were puzzled.

Then we heard a *whirring* noise.

WHHHIIIRRR budda budda budda whhhiiirrr...
It sort of sounded like a machine, but it also
sounded a lot like Vera just going *"whhhiiirrr,
budda budda".*

"This doesn't seem right," Laurence hissed.

"No," I agreed. I was beginning to wonder
whether Vera's time machine actually worked.

A bright beam flashed around the room. It
was very much like the light from Vera's torch.

"What's that, Vera?" Laurence asked.

"It's SCIENCE, Laurence. We are now travelling faster than the speed of light. We're hurtling back through minutes, hours, days, weeks, years, decades and centuries!"

"Are we?" Laurence said quietly. "It doesn't even feel like we're moving."

The torch-like light disappeared and the machine started shaking again. Then we heard *Bing bing bing... Bing bing bing*!

"And... *Bing!* We've arrived!" Vera announced.

"Do you think this might be a practical joke?" Laurence asked me softly.

"I'm not sure," I answered honestly. Right now I was as clueless as he was.

We unbuckled ourselves, hopped down from our seats and went to the back of the machine to meet Vera.

"Prepare yourselves for what happens next," she said in a serious voice. "We've travelled back many centuries and things may look and feel unfamiliar."

"Excuse me," Laurence said politely with one wing finger raised, "but I don't think we've gone anywhere." He folded his wings.

I nodded in agreement.

"Laurence, Marcus," Vera said patiently, "time travel science is *extremely* advanced and THIS machine has been designed to feel as smooth as possible. If you had experienced the full throttle of the speed at which we were travelling, well, all of your feathers would have fallen out, Laurence; and, Marcus, you would have shrunk to the size of a grain of rice."

"Oh no!" we both replied in unison.

Laurence hugged himself. "Have we really travelled back in time then?" he asked.

"Yes."

"Really, *really*?"

"Yes. Yes, we have."

"Gosh," he said.

I still wasn't sure whether to believe her but I didn't like the idea of being turned into a grain of rice.

Light was streaming into the wormhole from the forest. We climbed back up the ladder and found ourselves in a woodland clearing. It looked exactly like the clearing we'd landed in only a few minutes before.

Laurence gazed up at the trees.

"So are we in the past now?" he asked.

"You are indeed. We've travelled back in time approximately eight hundred years."

"Oh my!" he exclaimed. "LOOK! There's a tree, a *really* old tree!" He hopped to it and gave it a hug. "You're an old tree!"

"It looks the same as a modern tree, though," I said to Vera.

She stared deeply into my eyes and said in a kind yet pressing voice, "Trees have not really changed through the passage of time."

I felt funny inside. There was something wonderful about Vera. I wanted to follow her around and listen to everything she said and write songs about her.

She clapped her wings together. "Go and explore the woods. I'll wait here. Make sure you come back to the wormhole when you want to return home."

Laurence was ecstatic and hopped in a tight circle flapping his wings. "This is brilliant, Marcus! I can't believe we've gone back in time!"

He paused for a moment. "Let's explore the forest! We might see even more old trees!" And off he bounced rapidly out of the glade. I had to wriggle as fast as I could to keep up with him.

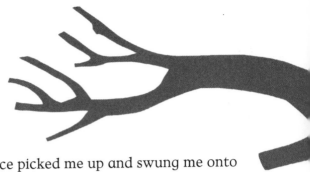

Laurence picked me up and swung me onto his back.

I had no idea what was really happening, but it was the happiest I'd seen Laurence in ages and that made *me* happy.

It was at that moment that we both saw a bird land on a branch. She was wearing very old-fashioned clothing, the sort that might have been worn eight hundred years ago.

I had the shivers.

It *really* was real.

We *had* travelled in time.

Chapter Nine

"Did you see that medieval bird?!" Laurence
asked, hopping from one foot to another.

"I did! Let's try and find another one!"
My cheeks were beginning to hurt from smiling
so much.

"Maybe we'll find a deer!" he hissed,
attempting to keep his voice low.

My eyes darted all around as we hopped

towards a dense crop of trees. I wanted to be the first to spot another woodland creature from the past.

"Ssshhh," Laurence whispered, stopping in his tracks.

"What?"

"Did you hear that noise?"

I stopped to listen. "It sounds like the cars on the motorway near our house."

"That's what I thought too."

"Did they have motorways back then?" I asked in a hushed tone.

"No. I don't think they had cars either." He shrugged. "It must be something else. Probably a babbling brook or a waterfall."

Without any warning a bushy-tailed figure suddenly somersaulted into our path.

"AAARGGHHH!" we both screamed.

It was a squirrel dressed in a fine woollen tunic. "Begging your pardon, I did not mean to startle you."

"It's a medieval squirrel," Laurence whispered discreetly out of the side of his beak.

"She looks like our friend J-Peg from home," I replied softly, copying his talking-out-of-the-side-of-the-mouth technique.

"Yes, she's got the same funny teeth."

"Maybe it's one of her ancestors."

"Why are you talking like that?" the squirrel asked. "I *can* hear you."

"Sorry, we didn't mean to be rude," Laurence mumbled, looking at his feet.

The squirrel didn't seem to mind too much and circled us with cartwheels. "Tell me, mysterious strangers, where have you come from?"

"We're from the future," Laurence announced proudly.

"The future?" she enquired, cartwheeling again. "I think you jest with me." She executed an impressive backflip that left her dangling upside down from a nearby branch.

"It's true," Laurence replied, taking a little hop to the right in an effort to imitate her energetic leaping.

"If you have travelled from the future, then you must be *very* hungry after such a long journey." She somersaulted back to the ground, landing squarely on her feet.

"I am a bit peckish, now you come to mention it," Laurence admitted sheepishly.

Laurence was always a bit peckish.

"In these woods at this point in history it is customary to *feed* peckish strangers," she laughed, before jauntily leaning against a tree. "And it just so happens that we have a special banquet prepared!"

"Really?" Laurence asked with a look of delighted disbelief.

"Yes! Follow me and we can eat and celebrate your arrival!" She sprang ahead of us, heading deeper into the forest.

"Ha ha! Okey-dokey! We'll be there in a minute!" Laurence called out loudly in a jolly voice. He turned to me. "I don't think we should go," he said seriously.

"We can't *not* go, Laurence. You've just said we'll be there in a minute."

"I think it's a trick. I've read about that sort of thing in my Robin Hood book."

Baffled, I stared at him. "What?"

"Robin Hood and his Merry Men would invite strangers to a banquet but then rob them. They were bandits."

"I thought Robin Hood was supposed to be a goody."

"He was."

"Robbing people doesn't sound very good or merry," I argued. I looked at the squirrel as she watched us from a distance, scratching her forearms nervously. I wondered if she might actually *be* Robin Hood. To my surprise, when Laurence wasn't looking, she suddenly winked at me. Why did she do that?

Was it some kind of medieval signal to say she was indeed Robin Hood? Or was it to say "Get a move on – your dinner's getting cold"?

"I think she probably *is* a bandit, Laurence. Shall we go home?" I suggested. "We've had fun time travelling. We saw all of those old trees and that medieval bird. That's probably enough of an adventure for one day."

"Hmm..." Laurence was thinking out loud. "But what if they *are* just being kind? I don't want to miss out on eating."

The squirrel seemed to realize that we weren't sure.

We didn't know you were coming, by the way. We always have a big lunch. Also, we're not bandits so you don't need to worry.

"Phew! That puts my mind at rest," Laurence sighed.

"I'm still not sure..."

But Laurence had stopped listening and was taking huge bites from a cheese sandwich that he'd pulled out from his feathers.

"What are you doing?"

"Just in case she is a bandit, I don't want her getting her paws on my sandwich," he gabbled with his mouth full.

"Come on, you two; everyone's waiting!" the squirrel shouted.

"We're coming!" Laurence cried, hopping towards her. I had no choice but to go with him, seeing as I was still on his back.

We can go back to the time machine if we need to, I thought to myself.

We followed a path through the woods that twisted and turned and led us to the most magical scene. Standing by a tree, beautifully dressed woodland creatures greeted us with warm smiles while a robin sang and played a melodic tune on her lute. Lanterns and flags hung from the branches, and in the fresh forest air there was an aroma of delicious home-cooked food.

"Is that spaghetti bolognese?" Laurence asked between sniffs.

"It is. Come and take a seat," the squirrel said, leading us to a table full of wooden bowls and silver platters overflowing with quiches, cheese sandwiches, bowls of broccoli, toast, mini fish pies, apples, lentil patties, ginger and courgette muffins, gherkins and much much more.

Laurence's beak fell wide open in disbelief. "But, these are all my favourite foods! I had no idea they ate such things in the olden days. This is like a brilliant dream come true!"

It was the biggest feast either of us had ever seen.

"I wish I hadn't eaten that sandwich now,"

Laurence whispered.

Chapter Ten

As we sat at the fancy banqueting table, a bird with a puffed-out chest stood behind us, refilling our plates every time we ate something. A crow was playing a flute as the woodland folk tunefully warbled and danced in circles.

"I can't believe this is happening," Laurence mumbled through a beakful of crisps. "I don't usually like parties, but this one is really good. It feels like we're in one of my history books."

I couldn't believe it either. Everything was working out perfectly, and all because of a few huge fibs that I'd told Laurence and some birds. I'd always thought telling lies was supposed to be a bad thing, but look at how everything had turned out. We'd actually travelled in a real time machine, Laurence and I were feasting like kings and everyone was having a fantastic time. I felt very proud of myself.

The serving bird put a slice of moist-looking banana cake on my plate. I closed my eyes and opened my mouth, ready to let it melt on my tongue. Instead of it being soft and sweet, however, it was hard, cold and lumpy.

"*Eeuw!*" I spat it out. "What *was* that? It tastes like vinegar!"

Laurence looked at the green lump on my plate. "I think it's a gherkin," he said. "You should try this – it's scrumptious."

Laurence was eating banana cake.

"Did you just do a switcheroo?" I asked crossly.

"I'm not sure. What's a *switcheroo*?"

"It's when someone secretly swaps things around and puts a gherkin on your plate when you were expecting a piece of banana cake."

"Yes, I did ... I thought you liked gherkins; you're always going on about them."

"I love gherkins, but not when they should be banana cake."

A worm who looked a little bit like my cousin Gavin interrupted our discussion to offer us some orange squash. As he filled my chalice he winked at me.

Why was everyone winking at me? Did everyone wink at each other in the olden days? Or did they all need glasses? I was just about to ask Laurence if not wearing glasses made people wink, when the squirrel stood up on a chair. She clanged a gong to attract everyone's attention.

"As you all know, we are celebrating the arrival of two very special guests, Laurence and Marcus, who have travelled here from the distant future."

Gdoing

The small crowd clapped and cheered. A caterpillar tooted a medieval party trumpet.

"To honour and welcome them we have made a special pie."

"They're very well organized, aren't they? It's almost as if they knew we were coming," Laurence whispered to me as a group paarp of sparrows wheeled out a gigantic pie.

I was getting a funny feeling in my tummy. Something wasn't right. How did the squirrel know our names? And why did everyone look so familiar...

"Ooh! Look at that!" Laurence cheered. "Is it a special medieval pie? It's got claws coming out of the sides."

"It's Mole!" screeched a bird who looked just like Laurence's friend Shakira in a piercing whisper. "He's not supposed to be here!"

← Stacey

Laurence and I both knew a mole from back home. He'd tried to cook us in a stew once. My worm heart began beating more quickly as I glanced around at all of the woodland folk.

I recognized every single one of them.

They *weren't* ancestors! They were our actual friends and neighbours. The squirrel was J-Peg, the worm that looked like my cousin Gavin *was* my cousin Gavin. Shakira and Bernard were there, along with ALL of our woodland neighbours, dressed up in medieval costumes.

We hadn't time travelled after all.

J-Peg

Bernard

Linda →

← Tanya

Vera must have somehow organized everything. But I didn't have time to think about how I admired her even more now, because the mole in the pie was noisily clawing his way out.

I had to act quickly. If Laurence recognized him – or any of our neighbours – he would realize that I'd lied about *everything*.

Geoff

← Sebastian

Chapter Eleven

The mole had burst his way out of the pie.

There was crust and mess all over the floor.

"Surprise! It's ME, Mole! You
forgot to invite me to
the party!"

Everyone looked horrified except for Laurence, who was clapping wildly and cheering with delight. "This is BRILLIANT! It's so much fun in medieval times!"

As Mole brushed his fur with his claws to get rid of the crusty pie pastry, Laurence studied Mole's face. He turned to me and whispered through a giggle,

"He looks just like that horrible mole who tried to eat us!"

"He's probably a very distant relative," I gabbled quickly.

"WHY IS EVERYONE STARING AT ME?" Mole shouted. "Come on, you lot – it's time to get the party started!"

"Oh, goody! Shall we play musical chairs?" Laurence cried.

"Great idea!" I yelled, hoping that dancing around some chairs might distract Laurence from noticing any more familiar faces. "Everyone, line up the chairs; you there, play us a tune," I said firmly to a pigeon with a violin. He nervously played "Twinkle, Twinkle, Little Star" at top speed, over and over again.

"Don't just stand there like lemons, you lot! Get moving!" Mole barked at everyone.

"Yay!" exclaimed Laurence, immediately hopping joyfully around the chairs. He was giggling. "I love this game!"

No one else wanted to play.

Mole grabbed a cockroach from the crowd. "Come and join in," he ordered. The cockroach did as he was told, skipping miserably to the tune. Mole shoved the creatures one by one towards the row of chairs.

"You as well, worm," Mole said, looking in my direction. He narrowed his eyes and scrunched up his face. "Don't I *know* you?"

Wanting to hear what Mole was saying, the pigeon stopped playing the violin. Everyone playing musical chairs dashed to claim a chair.

"Aw, we *all* get to sit down. There's supposed to be one missing," Laurence grumbled with disappointment.

"WE'VE DEFINITELY NEVER MET BEFORE, MOLE," I said a little unconvincingly.

"You're lying. I know exactly who you are."
Mole was making his way towards me; he looked
angry. The pigeon started playing "Twinkle,
Twinkle, Little Star" again, this time at twice the
speed. All the animals were frantically running
around the chairs trying to keep up.

Mole was just about to grab me with his long claws when Laurence shouted out, "Stop being horrible to my friend, you medieval meanie! He's NOT lying; we're from the future!" And, to my amazement, he plunged a huge ripe tomato onto Mole's head.

Everyone stopped what they were doing to watch the mole staggering about.

"What's happening? I can't see anything," Mole warbled angrily from inside the tomato.

"I've got a good idea," Laurence muttered to me.

"What is it?"

"Let's go back to the future before the mole takes the tomato off."

"OK," I agreed. Laurence flung me on his back and began hopping at full speed, along the forest path, heading back towards Vera's time machine.

I did think about telling Laurence that we hadn't really time travelled and that the time machine wouldn't be able to help us. But I decided to keep quiet.

phoo phoo

"I'm so glad we can get out of here," Laurence laughed with relief, "otherwise we'd be in big, big troub—"

"You ARE in trouble," boomed a sinister voice. "Big, BIG trouble!"

"Fly, Laurence, fly!" I screamed.

But it was too late. I felt a claw on the back of my neck...

Chapter Twelve

Laurence and I were being punished in a medieval way.

"I wonder if Vera is still waiting for us back at the time machine," Laurence sighed forlornly. "And even if she is, we're not going to be able to go back to the future now, are we?"

"I think we're going to be stuck here for a very long time," I said sadly. "Probably for ever."

Laurence didn't say anything for a while.

"At least we're together. There's no one else I'd rather be locked up with. You've been such a good friend, Marcus," he went on. "I still can't believe you let me come with you in your auntie's time machine. If I could put my wing on my heart, I would say that this is the most brilliant thing I've *ever* done."

He tried to put his wing on his heart, but couldn't quite reach, because of the stocks.

A lump rose in my throat. I felt awful. He thought I'd been a good friend, but if he knew how many lies I'd told him and the others, he'd think differently. I would never be able to tell him the truth now; it would break his heart. Also, he'd definitely be angry with me. It was my fault that we were locked up with no chance of escape. It was best to keep my worm lips firmly sealed.

Just then I heard footsteps and murmurings coming from the other side of some bushy shrubs.

"Do you think it's that meanie mole returning?" Laurence whispered in a panic. "He might do something even more horrible to us."

"What *is* going on in the woods?" asked a voice behind the shrubs. It didn't sound like Mole.

"I'm too scared to call for help," I whispered to Laurence. "It might be another baddie."

Laurence and I both strained to hear the conversation.

Another voice piped up. "You must be the only one who hasn't heard. Vera, that bird who runs the forest drama group, has put on a huge production. Loads of woodland folk have got involved to create a medieval banquet. Everyone rehearsed all through the night."

"Is that why there are strange objects all over the woods?"

"Yes. Bernard's made LOTS of props. They're very realistic. He's got a real talent for it..."

They were saying too much! I couldn't risk Laurence hearing any more.

"It's a bit rude listening to other people's conversations," I whispered. "Shall we sing a song instead?" I started humming.

Laurence tutted. "Quiet, Marcus! I want to hear what they're saying."

"But why did they do it?" the voices went on.

"It was for a bird from Oak Tree Woods. I can't remember his name now. Apparently he had a bump to the head and that made him obsessed with the idea of time travel."

"Who are they talking about?" Laurence asked.

"I'm not really interested. I'm too busy singing."

Tum te tummmm

tum te tum

"Was it that little round bird who looks like a chicken?"

"Yes, the one who's friends with a worm. The worm was the one who arranged it with Vera as a present for him. They're a very strange pair."

"Marcus, *stop* it!" Laurence was getting frustrated with my humming.

Hmmm mmmm

"*HMMMM HMM HMM!*"

"I think I know the one you mean. Is he the one who was convinced he was a flamingo?"

"That's him."

"Ah, yes, I remember now. Laurence. He's completely deluded, that bird, and gullible too. Fred said he didn't realize it was a play. He actually thought they'd time travelled."

"He didn't?! Ha ha ha! What an idiot!"

I didn't dare look at Laurence.

"They're talking about *me*, aren't they, Marcus!" Laurence wailed.

The animals heard Laurence's cry.

"We'd better go," one said before scurrying away.

Hmmmmm mmm mm mmm

There was a moment of silence. I gulped.

"What IS going on, Marcus?"

I laughed weakly. "Don't listen to those gossips. They're making up silly stories!"

"But they're not, though, are they?" Laurence said in a wobbly voice. "We *haven't* time travelled. It was all pretend. Vera made it all up..."

I didn't say anything. My cheeks were burning. I couldn't tell if Laurence was upset or cross; he was probably both.

"Admit it, Marcus," he said loudly. "You lied to me about your auntie inventing a time machine, didn't you?"

I nodded shamefully. "Yes, it was a lie."

"I KNEW it! And why did you tell everyone that I bumped my head?"

"I didn't want you to be disappointed that there wasn't really a time machine, so I told everyone the bang on your head made you think my auntie had built a time machine and you really wanted a go in it."

With great effort I turned to look at Laurence. His beak was wide open with shock.

"Vera told me she'd sort it out. I thought she was a magical wizard and so I went along with it. I didn't realize it was a play either."

Even though he seemed more than a little taken aback, it was a relief to be able to tell Laurence the truth at last. I wished I'd told him sooner! Having such a big secret had felt like I was wearing an invisible coat that was made out of concrete and iron, really heavy and uncomfortable. But now I felt as light and free as a butterfly doing ballet. I was filled with gratitude that he was taking this so well. He was an amazing friend; he was always patient, calm and understanding.

"I CAN'T believe you lied to me AND everyone in the forest!" he exploded in a not very patient, calm or understanding way. "Everyone now thinks I'm a fool. They're all laughing at me. How could you DO this to me?"

I tried to explain. "I really didn't mean for it to turn out like this, Laurence..."

"I don't want to hear any more. You're a lying traitor. And now I'm locked up with you in this thing *for ever*."

"I'm really, really, really sorry, Laurence, for lying to you. And I'm sorry for hurting you. I wish I could undo this whole mess."

Laurence didn't say anything. He turned his head away from me.

Knowing I'd upset Laurence so much made my heart hurt. I felt like a field ploughed by a tractor. There was nothing I could do to stop Laurence being upset with me. Not even the time machine could help because it wasn't real.

Birds sang in the distance. An aeroplane flew

overhead. A couple of large leaves fell noisily from a tree.

"Aren't you going to speak to me any more?" I squeaked.

"No, because you're a liar, liar and your pants are on fire."

I flipped from feeling like a sad ploughed field to feeling very cross.

"Well, Laurence," I burst out. "I only did it because I was fed up of watching you sit around on the sofa every single day like a great big lump of mashed potato."

"What's that supposed to mean?" he asked, raising his voice.

"You never want to do anything fun any more."

"Yes, I do! I make sure we do crossword puzzles every single day!"

"I don't WANT to stay at home doing stupid crossword puzzles."

"I thought you LIKED doing them! You always know the answers."

"I just want to go out and have adventures and fun, and for us to enjoy being together like we used to."

"Why didn't you SAY something, then? It would have been much, much easier than getting everyone in the forest involved in your ridiculous stories."

"I DID say something. YOU DIDN'T LISTEN TO ME!" *I* was shouting now.

Laurence was about to shout back when, without warning, an unidentified flying object fell from the sky and landed directly in front of us.

BLOOOMFF-SQUELCH!

BLOOOMFF

SQUELCH

Neither of us spoke as we studied the grey blob in front of us.

"Is it ... alive?" Laurence asked, forgetting we were in the middle of a momentous argument.

The blob raised its top end. "*Oooff!*" it whimpered.

"Yes, I think it is."

Chapter Thirteen

Laurence and I were watching the blob as it writhed on the ground when ...

BLOOOMFF-SQUELCH

and then

BLOOOMFF

...two more squidgy grey things fell from the sky and landed in the same spot.

"Are they ... slugs?" Laurence gasped.

"I'm not sure," I replied doubtfully. I didn't think slugs could fly.

The first blob lifted its head. "Is everyone all right?" it mumbled slowly.

"Yes," the others groaned.

"We'd better go and do that again," the first blob said. They all made moany-groany sounds as they flopped over onto their bellies.

"Excuse me, but what kind of creatures are you?" Laurence quizzed politely as they started to crawl slowly away, leaving a slightly disgusting trail of slime behind them.

They stopped and the first blob spoke. "We're slugs."

"Oh, you are? Are you a special *flying* breed?"

The slug spokesperson looked at us with a dazed expression. "We're not special. We didn't fly; we were flung here as part of the Slug Games."

"The Slug Games?" Laurence asked. "What are they?"

I was relieved that this unusual distraction had made him completely forget he was upset and angry with me.

"Yes, do tell us!" I joined in gratefully.

"I'm still upset and angry with you, Marcus, by the way," he reminded me.

The slug shrugged. "It's something Mole invented."

Laurence shuddered. "*Horrible* Mole?"

"Yes, him. He's got a catapult, and for fun, he fires us into the woods. The slug that flies the furthest is the winner."

"Do you enjoy that kind of thing?" Laurence asked.

"No!" they answered together.

"So why do you do it?"

They looked at Laurence as if he'd asked a very ridiculous question. "Because Mole is bigger than us. And he's scary."

"Oh! What a bully he is!" I piped up. "If I wasn't locked up in these stocks, I'd bop him on the head with his silly catapult."

"Yes!" Laurence agreed. "And I'd pick him up by his tiny little mole ears and send *HIM* flying!"

"Why?" the first slug asked slowly.

"Because he's being *horrible* to you. You don't deserve to be treated like that."

They looked at one another. "But we're *slugs*; no one likes us."

"You shouldn't be treated badly just because you're slugs."

They were all surprised. "That's the nicest thing anyone has ever said to us."

"It's a shame we're locked up, otherwise we'd definitely help you," Laurence said regretfully.

"Thanks for the kind thought. We'd better get back before Mole comes looking for us."

They began crawling away again. The smallest slug stopped and turned round. "Before we go, do you want us to help *you*?"

"There's nothing you can do. Mole locked us up and threw away the key," Laurence said matter-of-factly.

"It even has a lock!"

"That Bernard is very clever, isn't he!" the slugs marvelled.

Laurence managed to hold the tip of his wing aloft. "What do you mean by that?" he asked.

"They're not real stocks. Bernard made them out of cardboard for Vera's medieval production."

Laurence and I gasped. Laurence gave the stocks a little shake. The slugs were right: they *were* made out of cardboard and were very flimsy.

One of the slugs crawled over and took a nibble. The others followed, and Laurence and I watched in amazement as they gnawed the contraption. I'm not sure how long we stood there waiting for them to finish eating, but it felt like quite a long time.

"Eating cardboard is quite a treat!" one
commented with a little smile.

When they'd finished, Laurence picked me up and threw me into the air. "We're free, Marcus!" he cheered.

"Ha ha, we can fly home now!" I cried gleefully. I felt relieved and was even happier that Laurence didn't seem to be upset any more.

"So you're free," said a chilling, mocking voice behind us.

It was Mole. He was filing his claws while leaning against a hefty-looking catapult. "Are you going to bop me on the head with this catapult, little worm?" he sneered.

It didn't seem like such a good idea now that Mole was standing in front of me in real life.

"I didn't think so. You two are as pathetic as these slugs."

The slugs were crawling towards Mole for the next round of the Slug Games.

"Shall we just fly home?" I whispered eagerly to Laurence.

"No!" Laurence said firmly. "We can't leave these poor creatures with *him*. It's not US who are pathetic – it's YOU, Mole!" he shouted.

Mole clenched his sharp claws into fists. "What did you say?" he snarled menacingly.

What was Laurence doing? He was picking the wrong creature to stand around and have an argument with.

Chapter
Fourteen

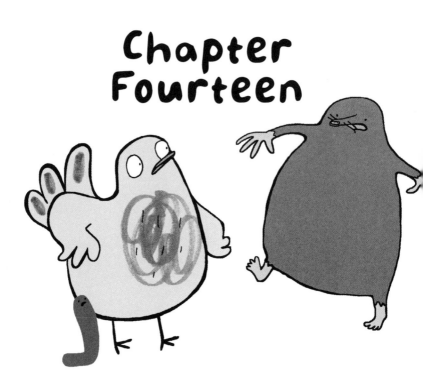

"You heard me, Mole. You're a sad, wretched bully and no one even likes you. You're only picking on these poor little slugs to make yourself feel better," Laurence stated bravely.

The slugs looked terrified. Part of me wanted Laurence to shut up, but the other part of me wanted to hear more. My friend sounded like some kind of mind doctor who understood the inner workings of a wickedly evil mole.

Mole waddled over to where Laurence and I were standing. I felt an overwhelming urge to burrow into the ground and dig one of my fantastic worm tunnels, but I didn't think now would be a good time to abandon Laurence. Especially as he'd only just got over his bad mood with me.

"If you want to play the Slug Games again, we're ready and waiting," a slug called out nervously from the catapult, trying to protect Laurence from Mole's wicked temper.

"You don't need to do the Slug Games any more. You can get down from there," Laurence called out with authority.

The slugs glanced uneasily at one another, unsure whether to do what he said.

"I said," he repeated, "get down from there!"

They quickly crawled back down to the ground and huddled together, trembling.

"So! I'm a bully," Mole whispered menacingly, millimetres from Laurence's face, "and no one likes me?"

"Mmm-hmm," Laurence agreed, and flinched. I couldn't tell if he was frightened or if he was being blasted by Mole's eye-wateringly bad onion breath.

"You're a fine one to talk," Mole seethed. "The only friend you have is a *worm*." He laughed, just like a proper baddie. "What kind of a ridiculous friendship is that? He's not even a real friend. He set you up to make you look like a fool in front of everyone."

"I didn't mean to, Laurence," I began to babble.

"Silence, worm," Mole commanded. He laughed again. "Mind you, it wasn't difficult to make you look stupid. Everyone knows how gullible you are." Mole was circling us now like a detective on a telly programme. "I need to choose your punishment very carefully. Perhaps I'll fire *you* out of the catapult too, just like those slugs you pretend to care about."

"Laurence has got wings; he can fly away any time he wants to," I said defiantly.

Mole stepped back. "Go on, then – do as your little worm friend says," he said softly, flapping his arms mockingly. "Fly away."

Laurence didn't move. "The slugs can't fly away from you, so neither will I. I'm staying here in support of my non-winged friends."

"See what I mean?" Mole lowered his gaze to stare at me and tapped my forehead with a pointy claw. "Your bird friend doesn't have much going on up here, does he?"

Mole picked up a long piece of ivy from the forest floor and began to tie Laurence's wings behind his back. Laurence didn't even try to stop him. Instead he closed his eyes and held his head high with an air of mysterious dignity.

"Ha ha! There! You can't fly away *now*," Mole sneered. "You really are just like one of your non-winged friends. Get over there with the slugs, the pair of you."

"You're right, I'm not very clever," Laurence exclaimed theatrically as Mole marched us over to the catapult. I glanced at him and he gave me a wink. Not another creature winking at me!

"I'm so *stupid* that I don't even know the answers to my own crossword puzzles. I always have to ask Marcus to help me."

I still had no idea what was going on. I was clueless.

"For example, right now I'm stuck on 1 down." He winked again. "It's ten letters, and the first letter is S."

I'd got it! Laurence was speaking to me in a secret code! Tingles ran down my back.

"And the clue," he went on, "is *when a banana cake becomes a gherkin.*"

Straightaway I knew the answer to Laurence's cryptic clue: *switcheroo*. He was talking about earlier when he swapped my gherkin for banana cake at the medieval banquet. I knew EXACTLY

 what he wanted me to do!

"We don't want to hear about your stupid boring crossword puzzles. Get in that catapult, all of you!" Mole demanded. "I'm going to fire the lot of you so far away, you'll never find your way home!"

"Your silly machine can't do that," I scoffed.

"Yes, it can. Get in."

"It's definitely not strong enough to hold all of us," I argued. "It's just made out of cardboard. It's going to break."

"It IS strong enough and it's NOT made from cardboard," Mole yelled crossly. "I should know: I made it myself!"

I gasped dramatically. "You didn't make *this*. It's *too* good."

The mole tried unsuccessfully to hide a proud smile. "I DID make it. I made it ALL by myself."

"Wow!" I gushed. "It's quite impressive." I looked the machine up and down and wriggled around it to admire it from every angle. "How does it work exactly?"

By now, the slugs were looking confused and extremely anxious.

Mole became animated, thrilled by my interest.

"Let me show you! First, you put a slug in like this." He lobbed the smallest slug into the bucket and leapt over to a wooden wheel. "Next you spin this to pull back the load, and then—"

I cocked my head to one side and pulled an unimpressed face.

"What's wrong?" he asked.

"That slug is too light. I don't believe the bucket can hold a heavier load."

"It CAN."

"Really?" I said in my most disbelieving voice.

"Yes, I'll show you with Laurence." He tossed the poor slug out and picked Laurence up.

I shook my head.

"Still not heavy enough?" he asked with a sigh.

"We need a more solid creature for the demonstration," I argued, looking around for a suitably solid creature.

"I know!" Mole said with excitement. "*I* could get in to show you."

"Hmm. That's not a bad idea," I replied casually.

Mole enthusiastically clambered up into the bucket.

"And then do I spin this wheel?" I asked.

"Yes! And as you can see, that pulls the bucket back like so," Mole called down. "The catapult uses tension, torsion and gravity to fling a load into the air – it's basic physics!"

The catapult creaked and groaned with the weight of Mole pulled back tight.

"And how do you release the load?" I asked innocently.

"By spinning the wheel the other way. But don't do that *now* or else *I'll* be fired away."

"Fire away, did you say?" I asked, spinning the wheel back the other way.

"What? NOOOOOOO!!!" Mole screamed.

The bucket sprang back to the upright position, flinging Mole into the air at tremendous speed.

KERRPLUNNNGGGGGGGGGGGG!

We all watched with our mouths and beaks wide open as Mole rocketed high into the sky.

167

KERRPLUNNNG

"Ha ha! You did it, Marcus!" Laurence roared with laughter as he hopped from one foot to the other. "You did the switcheroo!"

"And you did a secret code!" I cheered.

"Will he come back to get us?" one of the slugs asked nervously.

"Not any time soon," Laurence said reassuringly. "He'll have landed miles away."

"We're free!" I cheered. "We can go home and speak in secret crossword code!"

Laurence scooped me and all of the slugs up in his wings. "Let's ALL go home," he announced. "We can ALL spend the evening talking in secret crossword code."

It felt snuggly and safe in the warm embrace of friendship. Suddenly I remembered the argument we'd been having.

"Laurence," I asked timidly, "are you still upset and angry with me?"

He embraced me tighter. "No," he said. "I don't think you meant to be a nincompoop and hurt my feelings."

"I really didn't. It all just got out of hand."

"And as it happened, we did have a brilliant adventure travelling back in time, even if it wasn't real."

"It felt real, though. I wish it WAS real. I'd go back and do that all again."

"Me too."

"I don't mean to interrupt," squeaked a little voice from Laurence's left armpit, "but can you put us down, please?" It was one of the slugs.

"Oh! Sorry." Laurence carefully placed the slugs back on the ground.

"Thanks for helping us," they said politely, "and for inviting us around to your house. Maybe we could do that *another* time. We'd quite like to go home now."

We said our goodbyes and watched them crawl away, their trails of slime glistening magically in the afternoon sunshine.

"Do you think they *will* come around another time?" I asked.

"Probably not," Laurence said. He sighed with satisfaction and then yawned. "Shall we go home and make a vegetable pie?"

"Three letters, beginning with Y and ending with S," I answered in crossword code. "The clue is *the opposite of no.*"

Laurence didn't know what I was talking about. We flew home.

We didn't get round to making our pie that evening. Instead we talked and talked about everything, and only stopped when Laurence fell asleep, beak first, into his mug of hot chocolate. We'd been up all night.

Chapter Fifteen

The next few weeks were a blur.

Vera's medieval banquet play had been so popular that she decided to repeat it every day. Forest creatures came from far and wide to take part and experience *The Time-Travel Machine*.

Laurence and I joined Vera's drama club and we even organized our own shows. I did *The Worm Experience*.

Laurence did a *Fly Me to the Moon* performance.

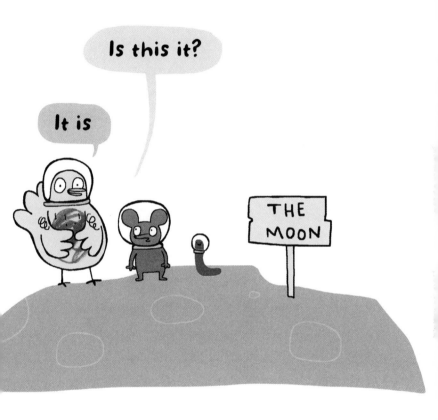

For some reason these weren't as popular as the medieval banquet.

No one has seen Mole since we catapulted him into the sky. Sometimes I wonder if he landed so far away that he had to start a completely new life. I hope he's not so horrible these days.

The slugs never did take up Laurence's invitation to come over to the house for a speaking-in-secret-crossword-code evening. They are too busy being famous. One of the slugs wrote a book about their experience with Mole, and now they spend their time giving talks in schools and libraries.

They even appeared on a daytime chat show.

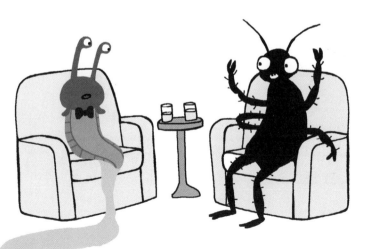

Laurence and I have become good friends with Vera. She comes to our house every week and sits on the sofa. Sometimes we don't even say anything; we just look at one another. At other times Vera will tell us stories about her life or other animals. These stories really make you think.

Even though she isn't a wizard, there is something magical about Vera. She brings out the best in both of us and inspires us to try new things.

Sometimes when Vera comes to the house she helps us talk and listen to each other about the things that really matter to us.

It makes a big difference and means that we don't get on each other's nerves as much.

Laurence and I leave the house a lot more these days and we've started having adventures again, just like we used to. Laurence has also been going out on his own, meeting up with his friends. He'll often go to the zoo with J-Peg, Shakira and Bernard. I'll go out digging on my own and make elaborate and fancy worm tunnels. One of the fun things about *not* spending time with each other is that when we meet up again, we have loads of new and interesting things to talk about.

These days I hardly notice when Laurence
is breathing noisily or making disgusting beak-
clearing sounds. Even when he is being annoying
I still really like him. I really, really like Laurence,
and before all of this happened I didn't even know
it was possible to care about someone this much.

Laurence hasn't touched his crossword puzzle
books in ages. He is too busy doing other things
these days. He read the quilt-making book and
made a beautiful quilt for my auntie.

Since meeting my actual auntie, Laurence has been studying his quantum physics books. He's decided that he is going to be the first bird to build a real time machine. I really think he can do it.

Until that happens, we'll keep having our adventures.

Thanks

With special thanks to my husband Tim, for his amazing kindness, support and belief in me. Thank you for looking after our little AJ so beautifully whilst I wrote and drew the pictures for this story.

Thanks to everyone at Walker Books, especially Lizzie, for the adventures we've shared whilst bringing Marcus and Laurence to life.

Thank you to Grandma, Da and family, Madeleine, Liv, Gabriel, Hilary, Becky and Evie for your encouragement.

And a squeaky shout out to Berwyn, Indi, Lois and Ivy.

About the Author

Award-winning artist and writer Simone Lia began painting and drawing in her dad's tool shed at the age of thirteen before going on to study at the University of Brighton and then the Royal College of Art. She writes The Simone Lia Cartoon – a weekly comic strip published in *The Observer* – and has written weekly comics for numerous publications, including *The Independent on Sunday* and *The Phoenix*.

She has written and illustrated several books for children and adults, including her debut novel *They Didn't Teach THIS in Worm School!* and the graphic novels *Fluffy* and *Please God, Find Me a Husband!*

Simone lives and works in London.